passover

passover

HarperCollins*Publishers*

HarperCollins*Publishers*
77–85 Fulham Palace Road, London W6 8JB

First published in the United States of America
by St. Martin's Press, New York.
First published in Great Britain
in 1996 by HarperCollins*Publishers*

1 3 5 7 9 10 8 6 4 2

A catalogue record for this book is
available from the British Library

ISBN 0 00627 997 X

Printed in Great Britain by
HarperCollinsManufacturing Glasgow

For Clara

David Mamet

Illustrations by
Michael McCurdy

"It was the mortar," the child said.

"That's absolutely right," the old woman said. "Now, do you know what mortar is?"

The child looked down at her hands.

"*Mortar*," her grandmother said, "is a substance to bind bricks. To bind them together." She took her hands and placed

1

them flat, the palm of one on the back of the other. They made a soft "clap," and the child nodded in agreement at the sound.

"So, it was the mortar, you see, which held bricks."

"What did the bricks build?" the child said.

"The bricks, they built—well, I suppose they built the pyramids."

The child made a slight moue, as if to say, You learn something new every day.

Her grandmother pushed the box of raisins down the counter toward the girl.

"Tradition, you see?"

The little girl had halved the apple and then carefully cut out the core. She put the flesh down and sliced through the red half-dome, five or six times. And then she turned it, and began to cut it crossways.

"That's right. Who taught you that?" the old woman said. "Your mother?" The little girl nodded.

"Well, she did a good job," the old woman said.

"Now, you know, we're making *our sort.*" She gestured to the ingredients out on the counter.

"And Aunt Yaffa will be bringing her contribution, which is the Sephardic kind." The two nodded slightly, pleased with their tolerance. "And there are, of course, *other* kinds, made from other ingredients. But this is the way that we make it in our family."

She saw the little girl give each ingredient a look, to rehearse it in her mind. As if she were bowing slightly to each, in its turn. "Apples and raisins. Walnuts. Honey. Wine…"

"When I was small," the old woman said, "my mother would serve apples and honey to me. Much as you see here. When we would study the Torah. And that was traditional, too.

"Now, in the *cheder,* long ago, did you know, when they went to school, three years old. Their father would wrap them up in his *tallis* and take them to *cheder.* They would be given little wood blocks. Of the *alef-bet,* which would have honey on them."

"The *alef-bet*..."

"That's right," she said.

"Of course it was just the boys, in those days." She wiped her hands on the white apron. "Are your hands sticky?"

"No," the girl said.

"Good. Here." She passed the jar of wal-

nuts to the girl. "Not too fine," she said.

The girl nodded and opened the jar. First setting the knife down carefully, perpendicular to the counter edge.

"Only the boys...But my mother was different. As her mother was. Which is why she taught us Torah.

"*She*, you understand, had learnt it in the Old Country, where they were more in the sway of tradition—

"So it was, with *her* family, I believe, even more than with mine, an accomplishment."

"To teach the girls...?"

"That's right."

The little girl nodded.

"And this is the same Clara who did that with the bird?" she said.

"That's right." How can they understand? she thought. They can't. Thank God.

"Tell me the story again," the little girl said.

"Who told you the first time?"

"Cousin Harold."

"Cousin Harold…" the old woman said. She looked down at the girl. "You use the knife very well."

"My mother taught me," the girl said.

"And the raisins," she said.

"Now?"

"Well, any time, if you will, but now, that will do."

The girl took the box of raisins and shook them out onto her hand, and then into the bowl. She looked to the old woman for approval.

"*Roshinkes mit mandelen,*" the grandmother said.

"What is that?" the child said.

"Raisins and almonds. That's a European song."

The girl nodded. "Was it that knife?" she said, and leaned toward it, as if she'd never touched it, as if it were an artifact.

The woman watched her for a moment.

"Was it that knife?" she said.

"No. But a knife like that. All right. Long ago…"

"…not this knife…" the child said to herself.

"…for, I was going to say that everything was lost. When they came over. But, of course, not *everything* was lost…."

"We still have the candlesticks," the little girl said.

"Yes, we do," the woman said. "We still have them."

"Whose were they?"

"They were, let me see—they were your great-great-great-grandmother's," the woman said.

The little girl glanced toward the dining room. She turned back. "And how did they keep them? All of these years? When they came over?"

"How did they keep them? They just did."

"But they didn't keep the knife...."

"You will find," the old woman said, "that objects..." She looked down at the little girl, chopping the walnuts so carefully. She watched her for a while. She felt she could have watched her forever—until the pile of nuts was chopped, and she said,

"That's good enough. No, that's fine."

The girl looked down at the knife, and then turned it over solemnly and used the spine to sweep the nuts off the counter, into the bowl her grandmother held below it.

She looked up to her grandmother, who nodded at the bowl, and then at the plate of diced apples and raisins; the nod meant, Now, you know what to do.

"Objects," the little girl said.

"Yes. That's correct. You know, we had a

samovar. You don't know what that is. It is a kettle, of a sort. It heats water, and you can put a kettle *on* it. It came over from Russia, where they drink tea quite a lot." The woman smiled.

"Just like we do here," the girl said.

"Precisely. And it belonged to my grand-mother, and I cherished it, and one of your uncles took it and his wife at the time made it into a lamp, and then it disappeared from…"

"Where is it?" the girl said.

"I couldn't tell you. I wish that I knew."

"Would you make tea in it?" the girl said.

"Indeed I would," the woman said. "And, do you know, in the Old Country, they would drink their tea, drink it with sugar; but they would put the sugar cube in their mouth, between their teeth, and strain the tea through it."

The little girl mixed the cut apples and the raisins in with the nuts.

"What cube?" she said.

"What cubes? Sugar cubes," the woman said. "You don't know what a sugar cube is.

"Sugar," she said, "used to come in little cubes. You see? About this big. Little cubes, wrapped up in paper. When you went to the coffeeshop, or a restaurant, when you were small, you could take them and stack them, and build with them. Walls. Or houses. Corrals for your horse, if there were enough, though there never were, of course. And, if you built a house, it was always a question, what you would use for the roof." She got down from the stool and went to the end of the counter and brought back the widemouthed jar of honey.

"What would you use?" the child said.

"A napkin, many times," the old woman said. "Though that was never completely satisfactory. Although I'll tell you one thing…"

"Uh huh…"

"If you had enough cubes, do you see, you could build up the walls until they only lacked a roof; then you could take your napkin, if it was a paper napkin, and fold it to make it stiffer, and lay it over the walls, do you see, so your house had a flat roof. Then you would use more sugar cubes to weight it down, do you see? So, in effect, you'd have a flat-roofed house with a small parapet. And it would look like a house in the desert."

"A desert house," the child said.

"That's right."

"Why do they have flat roofs?"

"We have steep roofs in the North," the woman said, "so snow falling on the roofs will not accumulate. Where it's hot, the roofs are flat, in many cases, to catch water."

The child nodded.

"And I'd fantasize," the woman said, "that's right, that it was a house in the desert. By some oasis. And the table, of course, was the desert sand, 'which stretched far away.' And, do you know,

when you look at them, they do not look
that different from the sugar-cube houses.
What do you make of that?"

"Houses in the desert?"

"That's right."

The child struggled with the honey jar,
and the old woman refrained from offering
help.

They sat in the afternoon light in the
kitchen.

The woman reached under her apron,
into the pocket of her housedress. She took
out a cigarette and a wooden match. She lit
the cigarette, and held the match under the
running tap. Then she held the charred end
briefly, and dropped the match into the
wastebasket at the foot of the stool.

In the wastebasket were peelings of
apple and apple cores. There was a teabag

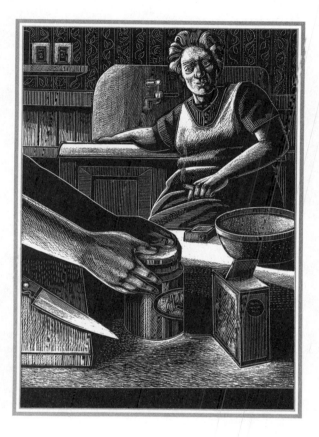

from her morning's tea, and a crust of toast. She looked down into the wastebasket, then raised her head, pinched the bridge of her nose, and sighed. She took a drag on her cigarette.

"They looked like that," the child said.

"I'm sorry, darling…"

"…the houses."

"They looked like what?"

"The *desert* houses…When you went there…?"

The woman thought, "sugar cubes." "Yes," she said, "they looked very much like that."

The child spooned honey into the bowl. One large wooden spoonful, and then another. She looked at her grandmother for direction.

"Go on," the woman said.

"And were you surprised?"

"…was I surprised? That they resembled my vision of them?"

"Yes."

"A bit, I suppose. I don't know."

"And were there camels?"

"There were some camels, of course."

"Did you ride them?"

"I remember mainly trucks."

"*Trucks…*" the little girl said.

"That's right."

The little girl nodded. She mixed the honey into the fruit and nuts. Then she looked up. The old woman nodded, meaning, Yes, that's enough, and the girl wiped the spoon off on the rim of the bowl several times.

"That's all right," her grandmother said. "No, you can't get it all."

"I hate to waste it," the girl said.

"Well, clean it off, no, don't worry; clean it off with your fingers. That's all right. Your hands are clean." She watched her. "Now put the spoon in the sink."

The little girl nodded. "And what was in the trucks?"

"In the trucks? *We* were in them," the woman said.

"…You were in them."

"That's right."

"Soldiers."

"Yes. That's right."

"…When you were in the *army,*" the little girl said.

"Yes."

The little girl looked down at the bowl, and then at her hands. She took the wooden spoon and walked to the sink, and began washing her hands. So serious, the woman thought.

"...But my *mother* wasn't in the army," the girl said.

"No. We were here."

"And was it an army like we have here?" the girl said.

"How do you mean?"

"...like..."

"Yes. Tell me."

"Like we see on television?"

"What do you...do you mean was there fighting? There was fighting, yes."

The girl finished washing her hands, and turned the taps off.

"Cloves," she said.

"No, I don't think so," her grandmother said, "but we *could*, I suppose...."

"No. I meant *cinnamon*."

"Yes, cinnamon," the woman said. "But we could use cloves, if you like." The girl nodded. The old woman reached up, took a small cellophane bag of cloves down from the cabinet, and handed them down.

"Not too *many* cloves," the little girl said.

"That's right. That would make it taste too strong."

"They'd make it taste like *soap*," the girl said.

"Mmm."

"...Do they have cloves in Aunt Yaffa's version?"

"...in her version? No. I don't know. I don't think so."

"What do they have?"

"They *have*..." she rehearsed it to herself, "...apples, nuts, honey..." She

31

frowned. "*Dates,*" she said. "Figs and dates. And that is what makes it different."

"Dates," the girl said.

"And it is more of a…'cake,' not a 'cake,' a…"

"…It's *thicker,*" the girl said.

"That's right. It…"

"…more like *mortar,*" the girl said.

"You're absolutely right," the woman said.

The girl reached forward on her stool, took the cellophane bag of cloves, and opened it. She shook several out onto her palm and looked at her grandmother, for her endorsement. The woman nodded. "Normally, they'd use crushed cloves. But, I think, if you merely *cut* one, and then stirred the mixture with the knife, there'd be the scent of cloves. What do you think?"

"I think so," the little girl said.

"Chop them a couple of times. And I think that will do." She dragged on her cigarette.

"How do you crush them?"

"With a mortar and pestle," the old woman said. "We had one of brass; and I remember, long ago, we had one of wood."

The little girl put a clove on the chopping block and cut it. The room filled with the smell.

"I think dates remind me more of the desert," she said.

"I think so, too," the woman said.

"If we had them, we could put them in."

"Of course."

"You said that this wasn't the same knife," the girl said.

"No. That knife was lost."

"Would you tell me about it?"

"…My *grandmother,*" the woman said, "had come back to their house on Erev Pesach. You see?"

"…she'd come back…"

"That's right. In the *shtetl.*"

"…she'd gone to the market."

"That's right. She had gone to the market. And she heard there that there was going to be an *attack*…"

"A *pogrom,*" the child said.

"Yes. A pogrom. That's right. She had… she had bought her ingredients, do you see, for the *Seder.* And she'd had to go back, for some last necessity…" The little girl nodded wisely. "…and I don't know what it could have been, the *Rabbi* might quiz you: the shankbone, the…I don't know…"

34

"…*matzoh*…" the girl said.

"It well could have been. '*Shmurah-matzo*,' do you know what that is?"

"Yes," the girl said.

"It could have been any number of things. And she had heard there, there was talk of a pogrom."

"They came at that time of year."

"Who told you that?" the woman said.

"…in school," the girl said.

"They told you in school?"

"That's right," the girl said.

"Did they tell you why?"

"…They said because of Easter."

The woman looked at her. "Well. That's right," she said.

"And so they were expecting it," the little girl said.

"Yes, and no. It may be right. They were

'hoping against hope,' but then they received the *rumor.* Somehow…"

"…They believed that it would happen," the girl said.

"That's right. So she stood there. Inside her house…"

"Where were the men?"

"Out in the field. Coming in. They would only work the half-a-day, of course.…"

"And would they go to the *mikvah?*" the child said.

"They might, or they might not," the woman said. "In any case, when she came into her house she was alone. And she stood," she said.

"As we are standing now. In her kitchen. Before the counter. With the makings of the Passover meal. And she looked

down. And she looked around.

"On the table were the two candlesticks, which she had put out. And she had dragged the bed to the tableside, for my grandfather. To recline. And all the makings of the meal were before her, and there was...*Just. Enough. Time...*" The child bobbed her head in rhythm to the last three words. "...to prepare the feast. And what was she to do? When they were coming to kill her. Her and her family?

"She stood there. The knife in her hand. She went to the bed. Where there were fine down pillows, and a featherbed. Do you know what that is?"

The child nodded, her dark eyes fathomless.

"...And she took the knife and she *ripped* it."

"…The bed?"

"…and the pillows, so that the down was everywhere. And she walked to the kitchen garden, and she took the chicken, the two chickens which would have been in the feast, and she took them in the house and cut their throats with the knife, and the blood spurted everywhere. On the walls, on the chairs, on the bed and the bedding, and she took the feathers, and she threw them in the blood, so that they stuck on everything they touched.

"And she took the knife, and reversed it. Holding it by the blade she walked out of the front of her house and, with the handle, broke in every window. Every pane. And when she came in her hand was bloody from the blood on the knife, and she made handprints all around the house.

"…as if someone… as if someone…

"And she hacked at the furniture with the knife, and threw it against the walls. And she emptied out the drawers of all her clothes, and ripped them. And she broke all the glass in the picture frames, and ripped up the books. Everything. And she tore down the pots and pans, and the pot rack. And ripped up the tablecloth, and dragged it in blood.

"When the men came home she was standing, clutching the candlesticks. She had dug a pit into the dung pile, back of the shed, in the kitchen garden. A pit, and a canvas cloth, with dung on top of it, and a small space underneath, for them to hide. In the dung heap.

"And they lay there, the two men, and her. That afternoon, and all that night.

While the villagers came through, they took the men away, and killed them, and took the women, and raped them, and tore the Jewish houses down, looking for those in hiding.

"But *her* house was spared."

That was the traditional end of the story. And the child nodded, and sat for a while. Then she looked over, past her grandmother, through the door to the dining room, where the table lay covered in the white tablecloth, with the two ornate silver candlesticks in the middle of it.

She looked back at her grandmother, to ask the question, and the woman nodded at her, "… that's right."

She took one last drag on her cigarette, and held it underneath the tap. She dropped it into the wastebasket.

They heard the sound of the key in the door. But neither moved. The old woman went to the child, and pulled her head toward her, and stroked her hair once, and again, and then kissed the top of her head: and then they both turned to the sound of activity in the entranceway.

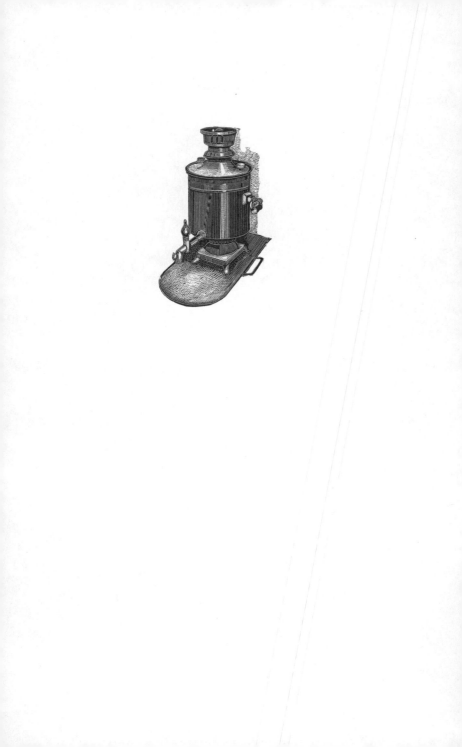